Although Oscar Wilde is best known for his plays, he was a man of many talents. Short stories, poems and novels came from his pen, together with some most delightful children's stories which are still popular nearly a hundred years later. Here are three of those stories, each one a classic in its own right.

First edition

© LADYBIRD BOOKS LTD MCMLXXXIII

THE HAPPY PRINCE

and Other Stories

Oscar Wilde

retold in simple language
by Marie Stuart

with illustrations by Gwen *and* Shirley Tourret

Ladybird Books Loughborough

The Happy Prince

There was once a prince who had
everything he wanted, so he was never sad,
and he never cried. Because of this, he was
called the *happy* prince. But alas, one day he
died. His people were sad about that, and
they had a statue made of him so that they
would never forget him. Although the statue
was made of lead, it looked just like the happy
prince, except that the eyes were made of
blue jewels and the clothes were of gold.
When the statue was ready, they put it on top
of a tall pillar in the middle of the town, where
everyone could see it.

Now in that country, the winters were very cold, and every autumn the swallows flew away to a warmer place where the sun shone. This year, however, one little swallow did not go with the others. He stayed behind at a place where reeds grew round a lake. The reeds were tall and graceful, and the swallow loved one of them so much that he could not bring himself to leave her. At last, when he saw that he was the only one left there, he said goodbye to her and flew off.

That night he came to the town and as he was tired he stopped to rest... where do you think? Why, on top of the tall pillar, right between the feet of the happy prince! The little swallow was just going off to sleep when a drop of water fell on his head. He looked up at the sky, but could see no clouds. Then another drop fell, and another. He looked up again and saw that it was not rain that had made him wet. It was *tears*! They were falling from the eyes of the statue!

"Who are you?" he asked.

"I am the happy prince," replied the statue.

"Then why are you crying?" asked the swallow.

"Because of all the unhappy things I can see in this town. When I lived in the palace I did not know anything about them. But up here I can see everything, and it makes me very sad."

"What can you see?" asked the swallow.

"Far off in a poor little street," said the prince, "there is a house with an open window. Inside the room a woman is sewing a beautiful dress for one of the queen's maids to wear at the ball. In a bed close to her lies her little boy. He is very ill and his mother has no

money to pay for a doctor to come. She has nothing to give her little boy but water. I think he is going to die. Little swallow, will you take her the red jewel from the hilt of my sword? She can sell it and buy food. I cannot take it to her because my feet are fixed to this pillar.''

"But I am on my way to the south," said the swallow. "All the others have gone. I shall be lost if I don't go soon."

"Please, little swallow, stop here just one night and do as I ask," pleaded the prince.

"I don't like boys very much," said the swallow. "Some of them throw stones at me."

"This one is very, very ill. *Please*, little swallow."

"All right. Just one night then."

So the swallow pecked out the red jewel and flew off with it in his beak. On the way he passed the big house where the queen's maid

lived. He heard her say, "I hope my dress will be ready in time for the ball. That lazy woman is so slow; she will have to work much faster or it will be too late."

The little swallow flew on till he came to the poor house. The boy was tossing about in his bed, but his mother had fallen asleep with her head on the table, she was so tired. The swallow hopped through the window and put the red jewel close by her thimble so that she would see it when she awoke. Then he flew over the sick boy's bed and fanned him with his wings.

"How cool I feel!" said the boy. "I must be getting better." And he fell asleep.

Back flew the swallow to tell the happy prince what he had done.

"It's a funny thing," he said, "but I don't feel cold any more."

"That's because you did a good deed," said the prince.

All the same, the swallow still wanted to fly away to the warm land where his brothers and sisters had gone. So that night he said to the prince, "Goodbye, I'm off now!"

"Little swallow," replied the prince, "don't go yet. I can see a poor young man in a bare room where there is no fire. He is trying to write but his hand is too cold to hold the pen. And he has no food to eat."

"Do you want me to take him another jewel from your sword hilt?" asked the swallow.

"There was only one," replied the prince. "You will have to take one of my eyes. They are made of blue jewels and cost a lot of money."

"But I cannot do that!" cried the swallow.

"Please do as I ask," begged the prince.

So the swallow pecked out one of the jewels from the statue's eyes and flew with it over the chimney pots, to the room of the poor young man.

He went in through a hole in the roof and dropped the jewel into a bunch of flowers on the table. When the young man saw it he thought someone had sent it with the flowers because they liked a play he had written. He was so pleased that he forgot he was hungry, and went on with his work there and then.

"Now I can pay my rent and buy some food," he said.

Back flew the swallow to tell the prince the good news. "And now, goodbye," he added. "I'll come back next spring and bring you a red jewel and a blue one to replace those you have given away."

"Don't go yet," pleaded the prince. "Look down there. Do you see that little girl? She was trying to sell matches but her hands were so cold that she has dropped them in the wet and now they are no use. Her father will beat her when she gets home. You must peck out the jewel from my other eye and give it to her."

"But if I do that you won't be able to see at all!" cried the swallow. "You will be blind."

"Please do as I say," begged the prince.

So the swallow took the blue jewel and put it in the little girl's hand. "How pretty!" she smiled when she saw it. And she ran off home to give it to her father. He would not beat her now.

Back once more flew the swallow. He said to the prince, "I cannot leave you now that you are blind. I will stay with you always, and you can use my eyes now that yours cannot see."

As the days grew colder, he told the prince all about the warm land where his brothers and sisters were living. As he talked, he did not feel quite so cold. But the prince wanted him to fly over the town and tell him what he saw. There were big houses where rich people lived, but there were many more dark lanes where poor people lived in ugly huts. Their children had thin, white faces because they did not get much food. One day, the swallow saw two little boys lying down under a bridge trying to keep one another warm. Along came a policeman and told them to go home — he did not know that they had no home to go to. They just got up and went out hand-in-hand into the rain.

When he heard this, the prince was very sad. "I have no jewels left," he said, "but my clothes are made of gold. You must peck off a bit and give it to those poor children."

Every day the swallow saw someone who needed help, and before long all the gold from the prince's clothes had been given away. He stood on the top of his pillar looking dull and grey, but the faces of the children were no longer white — their cheeks were red and their thin arms and legs grew nice and round. They began to play in the streets, and no longer had to beg for bread.

Then the snow came. The poor little swallow got colder and colder, but he would not go away from the prince. At last he knew that his end had come. "Goodbye, dear prince," he whispered as he fell at the statue's feet.

"Goodbye," replied the prince. And something broke inside him. It was his heart.

Next day the mayor and town councillors passed by the pillar and looked up at the statue.

"Dear me! How shabby our prince looks!" they cried. "He seems to have lost all his jewels and someone has stolen his gold clothes."

"And look! There's a horrid dead bird at his feet! We can't have that here! It must be taken away at once!"

"We'd better take the statue down too," said another councillor. "We'll put up a better one in its place. Whose shall we put there this time?"

"Mine, of course," said the mayor.

So they took down the prince's statue and melted the lead to make the new one. But the workmen found a broken heart inside, and that would not melt. So they threw it on the dust-heap where the little dead swallow was lying.

That night God told his angels, "Bring me the two most precious things in this town."

They brought Him the broken heart and the dead swallow. And God said, "You are right. So this little bird shall always sing in my garden of Paradise and the happy prince shall praise my name for ever."

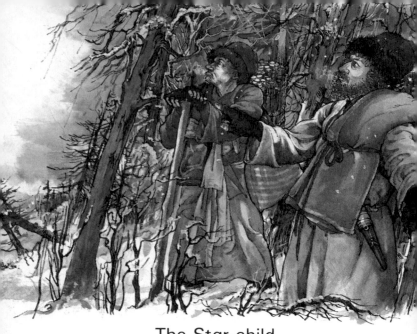

The Star-child

Once upon a time, two woodcutters were going home after their day's work. They were tired and very, very cold, for it was winter and the snow lay deep on the ground.

As they came out of the wood into the open, the sky was black overhead. Suddenly they saw a flash like lightning.

''Make a wish!'' said one woodcutter. ''That's a falling star — it brings good luck!''

''It fell into that bush over there,'' said the other. ''Maybe there is a pot of gold where it landed. The first to find it can have it!''

They both ran to the bush and looked about. There, lying on the white snow, they saw something that shone like gold. The first man to get there called out, "It's a white coat with gold stars all over it." He opened it to see what was inside, and there, fast asleep, was a baby boy. The man was disappointed, for he had been hoping to find a lot of money and be rich.

"I don't want any more children," he said. "As it is, we never have enough to eat. Let's leave this child here."

"We can't do that, it will die of cold," said the other man. He took it up in his arms, and carried it home. His wife opened the door, glad to see him again. When she saw that he had something in his arms, she asked, "What's that?"

"I found it in the forest," he said, showing her the sleeping child.

"Take it away!" she cried. "We have our own children. How can we feed another one?"

"This is a star-child," he replied, and told her how he had found it.

"Take it away!" she said again. "We can't keep it here."

The woodcutter knew that his wife had a
kind heart, and that she only said "No"
because they were so poor. So he waited. She
turned her back on him and went over to the
fire. The freezing wind blew through the open
door, and she thought, "How can I send that
child away on such a cold night?" Aloud she
said, "Close the door."

Her husband came in and placed the sleeping child in her arms. There were tears in her eyes as she gave it a kiss, then she put it in a cot next to her own baby.

Next morning they put the cloak with the stars on it in a box. There was also a gold chain round the star-child's neck, and they put that in the box too.

"We could sell these things to buy food," said the wife.

"They aren't ours," replied the woodcutter. "Maybe one day someone will come looking for the child, and then we can give them back."

So the star-child lived with the woodcutter and his wife just as if he were one of their own children. But the others all had black hair and black eyes, and *his* eyes were blue, his hair golden, and his skin as white as milk. He was very beautiful to look at, but he was not beautiful in his ways. He was always boasting to the woodcutter's children that *his* father and mother were a king and queen and that they lived on a star, not in a poor hut. He never helped anyone, and he always asked for the best of everything. He was very vain, too. Often he would lie by the well in the garden and look at his reflection in the water. Then he would smile and say, "How good looking I am!"

He was very unkind to the birds and other animals, as well. He threw stones at them, and laughed if he hit them. He really was a *horrid* little boy!

One day, a poor woman who was dressed in rags came to their village. She was so tired that she sat down under a tree to rest her feet.

"Let us drive her away, she is ugly and dirty," said the star-child, and he threw stones at her.

"STOP!" cried the woodcutter when he saw what the boy was doing. "She has not done you any harm."

"Don't talk to me like that!" shouted the star-child. "You can't stop me. I shall do it if I like. You aren't my father."

"No. But when I found you in the forest I brought you back here, and my wife and I have looked after you as if you were our own child."

The beggar-woman jumped up when she heard these words. "Did you say you found him in the forest?" she asked. "How long ago?"

"Ten years to this very day," replied the woodcutter.

"Did he have a gold chain round his neck? And was he wrapped in a white cloak with gold stars on it?"

"Yes," answered the woodcutter. "We put them in a box to keep them safe. Come in and see."

When the beggar-woman saw what was in the box, she cried, "This boy must be my son! Some bad men took him from me ten years ago, in the forest. I have been searching for him ever since. At last I have found him!"

The woodcutter's wife called to the star-child, "Come at once! Your mother is here!"

Joyfully the boy ran in. But when he saw the beggar-woman in her poor clothes, he shouted rudely, "That's not my mother! She's just an ugly beggar. Send her away!"

The poor woman held out her arms and cried, "You are my long lost son. Please come and give me a kiss."

"I would rather kiss a snake!" yelled the boy. "Get out of my way!" And he pushed her from him.

She went sadly back into the forest. The star-child went out to play with the other children. But they ran away from him saying, "Who are you? We don't know you! How ugly you are! Go away!"

"Why do they say that?" said the star-child to himself. "I know that I am beautiful." And he went to the well in the garden to take a look. What he saw gave him a fright! His beautiful face was now ugly like a toad's and his white skin looked like a fish's scales.

"Who has done this to me?" he cried. "It must be because I was unkind to that woman who said she was my mother. I must find her and tell her I'm sorry."

Away he went to the forest calling, "Mother! Mother!" as he ran. He asked the birds to help him to find her, but they said, "You used to throw stones at us. We don't like you!" and they flew away from him. So he went on looking till night came, then he lay down on a bed of leaves and fell asleep.

Next day he set off again, asking all the animals he met if they had seen his mother. The mole said, "How can I see? You put out my eyes for fun."

So next he asked a little bird, "Will you please fly up high to look? You will be able to see a long way then."

But the little bird answered, "You cut off my wing feathers, and I cannot fly far now."

And the squirrel said, "You killed *my* mother so why should I help you find *yours*?"

Beyond the forest he came to a village. Here all the children made fun of him and threw stones at him because he was so ugly. But he did not stop looking. On and on he went, from place to place, always asking for his mother, but no one could tell him where she was. Three long years went by in this way.

One night he came to a city with a high wall all round it. There were two soldiers at the gate, and they stopped him from going in. "What do you want?" they asked.

"I am looking for my mother," he told them.

They laughed at him, and one said, "I should think she was glad you are lost, you are so ugly. Be off with you! No one wants you here!"

Sadly he turned to go away, but an old man standing nearby said, "I will give you a bottle of wine for him. He can work for me."

"Done!" replied the soldiers.

The old man, who was really a magician, led the star-child through narrow city streets till they came to a little door in a wall. The magician took the boy inside and pushed him into a damp, dark cellar. He gave him a bit of bread to eat and some water to drink. Then he locked the door and went away, leaving the star-child all alone.

In the morning the magician came to him and said, "Hidden in a wood near this city, there are three pieces of gold. One is white gold, one is yellow gold and the third is red. You must go and find the white gold and bring it here to me. If you don't, I shall beat you a hundred times with this stick. Come!"

He opened the door and let the star-child out. "Be back here at sunset," he warned, "Now go!"

The star-child found the wood, for it was not far away, and began to look for the white gold. He looked everywhere, but he could not find any. The hours went by, and at last he saw that the sun was setting in the west. He would have to go back to the magician without the gold, and he knew that he would get a beating.

Just as he was leaving the wood, he heard a cry of pain. Even though it would make him late and the magician would be even more angry, he went back to see if he could help. He found a hare caught in a trap. "You poor thing," he said, opening the trap. "I will soon set you free."

"Thank you," said the hare. "What can I do for *you*?"

"I'm looking for some white gold," said the boy, "but I can't find any. If I don't take some to my master, he will beat me."

"Come with me," said the hare. "I know where there is some." He took the star-child to a tree where the gold was hidden in a crack in the bark. Thanking the hare, the star-child ran back to the city with the gold. At the gate he saw a poor beggar-man who cried, "Please give me some money to buy bread, or I shall die."

"I only have one piece, and I must take it to my master," said the boy.

"I have had no food for days. Please!" begged the poor man.

So the star-child gave him the white gold, and went back to his master with nothing. The magician was very angry. He took the boy back to the cellar and beat him, then left him to cry himself to sleep.

Next morning the magician came and told him, "Today you must find the yellow gold and bring it to me by sunset. If not, I will whip you three hundred times."

Again the boy hunted all day for the gold, but could not find it. When he saw the sun beginning to set, he sat down and cried. He was afraid to go back with empty hands.

"Why are you crying?" said a voice. It was the hare whom he had set free the day before.

"I have looked all day for some yellow gold for my master, but I can't find any."

"Follow me," said the hare, and he took the boy to a little pool. There, at the bottom of the water, shone the yellow gold. Thankfully the boy ran back with it to the city. As he ran, he saw the beggar-man limping along.

"Help! help!" he called when he saw the

star-child. "They have driven me out of the city and I have nowhere to go. I shall die of cold tonight. Please give me some money to pay for a bed."

"I only have one piece," said the boy, "and I must take it to my master or he will whip me."

But the man kept on begging, and in the end the boy gave him the piece of yellow gold. When the magician saw that he had nothing, he beat him harder and longer than the night before, and left him in the cellar with no food.

On the third morning, the magician told him, "Today you *must* bring me the red gold. If you don't, I shall kill you."

All day the star-child searched for red gold in the wood, but found nothing. When evening came, he sat down and cried. Soon the hare came along again, and told him to look in a little cave just behind him. There in a corner he found some red gold, and joyfully he set off with it. But he had only gone a little way when he saw the beggar once more. When the star-child saw how ill he looked, he was so sorry for him that he gave him the red gold too.

"Now it will be the end of me," he said, slowly making his way back to the city. When he came to the gate, the two soldiers who guarded it stepped forward and bowed, calling him, "My Lord."

He thought they were making fun of him, but as he went on through the streets, many people came crowding round him, saying to one another, "How beautiful he is!"

They would not go away, and there were so many of them that he could not find the door to the magician's house. Instead he saw a palace gate in front of him. Some men came out to meet him, saying, "We have been waiting for you, O beautiful prince."

"I am the son of a beggar-woman," he told them. "And I know that I am ugly. Why do you call me beautiful?"

Then one man held up his shining shield and said, "Look in this."

And the star-child saw that his face had once more become as beautiful as when he used to see it in the water of the well.

"You must be our king," the people said. "A wise man told us our king would come today."

"No, I must go. I am looking for my mother," he told them. "She is not a queen, she is only a poor beggar-woman." And he turned to go back towards the city gate.

And there, coming towards him, was the beggar-woman who had said she was his mother. With her was the beggar-man to whom he had given the three pieces of gold. With a cry of joy, he ran towards them. He knelt down at the beggar-woman's feet crying, "Mother, forgive me!"

As he knelt there, both the beggar-man and the beggar-woman placed their hands on his head, and said the one word, "Rise!"

He stood up, and when he looked at them, he saw that they were no longer beggars, but a king and queen, each wearing a gold crown.

"This is your mother," said the king.

"And this is your father," said the queen.

Then they both put their arms around him and kissed him. After that, they took him into the palace. They gave him beautiful clothes and placed a gold crown on his head because they said he was to be the king of that city.

The very next day, he sent rich gifts to the woodcutter and his wife and children. As for the bad magician, he sent him far away. And thereafter, as long as the star-child lived, no one in that city was ever poor or hungry, and they were all happy together.

The Young King

Just before the old king died, he sent for his grandson who was going to take his place. Until that moment, the lad had never seen his grandfather. This was because the old king had been angry with his daughter, the boy's mother, and had sent her away from the palace. She had gone into the forest, a long way off, and there her baby was born. She gave the baby to a poor man and his wife who lived in a cottage nearby. They were kind to him and looked after him as if he were their own son. Now he was sixteen years old and had become a tall, handsome lad.

When he came to the palace, he was dressed as a poor shepherd boy with a crook in his hand. He opened his eyes wide when he saw how beautifully all the men and women were dressed. Everything was very grand after the poor hut he had been used to. He gazed at the rich carpets and curtains, the pictures on the walls, the golden candlesticks, the silver vases full of flowers, the silk cushions and pretty ornaments.

He was pleased when they took away his old coat and shepherd's crook and gave him nice new things to wear.

''Now you look like a prince,'' they said. And indeed he did!

When they told him that he was to be their new king, he could think of nothing but what he would wear on the day that he was to be crowned. He wanted a robe woven of gold threads and a crown with red rubies. As for the sceptre which he would hold in his hand when he sat on the throne, it must have a ring of real pearls at the top. The night before he was to be crowned, he lay awake thinking of these things, and when at last he fell asleep he began to dream.

He dreamed that he was in a very big room where a lot of men, women and children were working. It seemed to be a kind of factory, and the people were standing at looms weaving cloth. They were poor and dressed in rags. Children sat under the looms so that they could tie the ends of the threads with their tiny fingers if any of them snapped. They had white faces and thin arms, and they looked as if they did not get much to eat. The room was noisy with the clatter of the looms, but no one was talking or laughing. The young

king stood close to one of the weavers to see what he was doing.

"Why are you looking at me?" asked the man. "Has our master sent you to spy on us?"

"Who is your master?" said the young king.

"He is a man like me, but he has fine clothes to wear while I go in rags. He has more food than he can eat, but my children go hungry," replied the man.

"Why do you work for him then?" asked the young king. "You are not a slave."

"You think I am free," replied the man, "but I am like a slave because I am poor. I must do this work or starve."

As the man talked, he did not stop weaving. The shuttle flew to and fro and the young king saw that the thread was of gold. "Who is this for?" he asked.

"For the young king who is to be crowned tomorrow," replied the man. "We must work fast or it won't be done in time."

When the young king heard this, he cried out to the man to stop. That woke him up. He saw the moon shining through his bedroom window so he knew it was still night. He turned over and went to sleep again. Once more he began to dream.

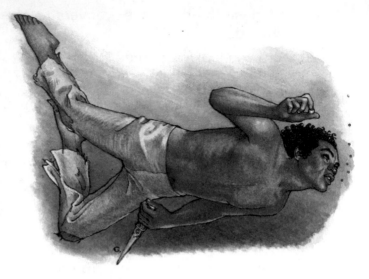

This time he was on the deck of a ship,
which was being rowed by a hundred black
slaves with chains on their legs. In the middle
sat a man with a long whip. If a slave stopped
rowing even for a moment, he whipped his
bare back. Soon they came to a little bay, and
here they dropped anchor and took down the
sail.

Then one man was made to dive into the
sea. When he came up he had a pearl in his
hand. The master of the galley took it from
him and, with a crack of his whip, made him
dive again. Each time the man came up with a
pearl, the master took it and put it in a little
bag. Over and over again the poor man dived.

Each time it took him longer, and each time he came up he looked more tired. The last pearl he brought up was the biggest and best. The master took it from him, saying, ''This will be in the centre of the ring of pearls on the young king's sceptre, tomorrow!'' Then he told his slaves to pull up the anchor and row as hard as they could. They left the diver behind — because he had died.

In his sleep the young king gave a loud cry and woke himself up. But he saw the stars in the night sky through his window so he went back to sleep, and dreamed again.

43

He dreamed that he was alone and walking
through a wood. Then he came to a place
where there had once been a river, but it was
now dry and there was no water in it. Here, in
the river-bed, were hundreds of men hunting in
the sand. The sun beat down on their heads
and they seemed to be very tired, but they did
not stop. He could not see what they were
looking for, but every now and then a man
would fall down, and not get up again. This
happened many times, and the young king
knew that they were dead. Then black
vultures came flocking in the sky overhead,
and out of the slime and mud at the bottom of
the valley came dragons and horrible snakes.
The young king was afraid.

"Who are these men and what are they
looking for?" he called.

"They are trying to find red rubies for a
king's crown," replied a voice behind him.

He turned round and saw a man with a mirror in his hand. "For what king?" he asked.

The man held up the mirror. "Look — and you will see him," he said. When the young king saw his own face, he gave a loud cry and woke up once more. Now it was morning, and the sun was shining through the window.

Then into his bedroom came the officers of state. They bowed to him and called the page boys to bring in the robe of gold thread, the crown and the sceptre for the young king to see. He looked at them and saw that they were very beautiful. Then he thought of his three dreams and said, "Take these things away! I will not wear them."

They thought he was saying that for fun so they did not go. But he said again, "Take them away! This robe was woven on the loom of pain. There is blood in the heart of the ruby, and death in the heart of the pearls." And he told them his three dreams.

They looked at one another and said, "He must be mad! A dream is only a dream. What has that to do with these things?"

And one said to him, "My lord, you must put on this robe. How will the people know that you are our king if you do not dress like one?"

"Is a king only a king when he wears a crown?" asked the young king. "I thought he must *always* be a king in his ways. But you may be right. Anyway I will not wear this robe, nor will I be crowned with this crown." And he sent them all away, except for one page boy.

"Please bring me the clothes I wore when I first came here," he told him. Then he put them on and took the shepherd's crook in his hand.

"But, my lord, you have no crown," said the page boy.

So the young king picked a spray of the red roses that were growing round the window of his room. He bent it into a circle and put it on his head. "This is my crown," he said.

Then he went into the great hall where all the nobles were waiting for him. When they saw him they cried, "My lord! The people wait for their king, but you look like a beggar. You bring shame on us all."

He did not answer them, but walked down the stairs and out of the gates. Here he got on his horse and rode to the cathedral. The little page boy ran beside him.

All the people in the street laughed and said, "It is the king's fool! He is playing a joke on us!"

But the young king stopped his horse and said to them, "No, I am your king." And he told them his three dreams. They did not understand him, and one man said, "How will it help us if you don't wear the gold cloak? Rich men make work for us poor ones, and if we can't work, we starve!"

"There must be a better way, and I will find it," replied the young king. And he rode on.

When he came to the great porch of the cathedral the soldiers who were on duty stopped him saying, "You can't go in. No one can enter by this door but the young king."

"I *am* your king!" he replied, and pushed their swords aside.

The bishop who was waiting to crown him said, "Why do you come dressed as a beggar? I cannot crown you until you put on your gold robe."

49

"How can you say that in this house?" replied the young king. "Do you forget that our Lord was the son of a poor carpenter and born in a manger?" And he told the bishop his three dreams.

"My son," said the bishop sadly, "I am an old man and I know that there are many bad things in this world. But you cannot stop them. So go back and put on the gold robe, then I will crown you and put this sceptre of pearls in your hand."

The young king strode past the bishop and went up the steps of the high altar. There he knelt to pray with the white candles burning around him. And while he knelt, soldiers came in with their swords, shouting, "Where is this beggar king? Kill him! He is not fit to rule over us!"

Then the young king rose to his feet and turned to face them. And lo! through the stained glass windows the sunlight streamed upon him and the sunbeams wove about him a robe that was much more beautiful than the golden robe that had been made for him. The shepherd's crook that he held in his hand blossomed with lilies that were whiter than the pearls in the sceptre. And redder than any rubies were the roses in the crown that he wore upon his head.

As he stood there, looking every inch a king, the soldiers put up their swords and knelt in awe. The bishop said, ''One greater than I has crowned you.''

Then the trumpets sounded, and as the choir-boys burst into song, the young king came down from the high altar. But no man dared to look upon his face, for it was like the face of an angel.

Stories . . . that have stood the test of time

SERIES 740
FABLES
A first book of Aesop's Fables
A second book of Aesop's Fables
Aladdin and his wonderful lamp
Ali Baba and the forty thieves
Famous Legends (Book 1)
Famous Legends (Book 2)
La Fontaine's Fables:
The Fox turned Wolf
Folk Tales from around the World

Ladybird titles cover a wide range of subjects and reading ages.
Write for a free illustrated list from the publishers:
LADYBIRD BOOKS LTD Loughborough Leicestershire England